Welcome to the Forest, where
THE MINISTRY OF MONSTERS
helps humans and monsters live side
by side in peace and harmony...

CONNOR O'GOYLE
lives here too, with his gargoyle mum,
human dad and his dog, Trixie.
But Connor's no ordinary boy...

When monsters get out of control,
Connor's the one for the job.
He's half-monster, he's the Ministry's
NUMBER ONE AGENT,
and he's licensed to do things
no one else can do. He's...

MONSTER BOY!

First published in 2009 by Orchard Books
First paperback publication in 2010

ORCHARD BOOKS
338 Euston Road, London NW1 3BH
Orchard Books Australia
Level 17/207 Kent St, Sydney, NSW 2000

ISBN 978 1 40830 245 3 (hardback)
ISBN 978 1 40830 253 8 (paperback)

Text and illustrations © Shoo Rayner 2009

The right of Shoo Rayner to be identified as the author and illustrator of this work has been asserted by him in accordance with the Copyright, Designs and Patents Act, 1988.

A CIP catalogue record for this book is available from the British Library.

1 3 5 7 9 10 8 6 4 2 (hardback)
1 3 5 7 9 10 8 6 4 2 (paperback)

Printed in Great Britain

Orchard Books is a division of Hachette Children's Books,
an Hachette UK company.

www.hachette.co.uk

MONSTER BOY

OGRE OUTRAGE

SHOO RAYNER

ORCHARD BOOKS

"This bike's pathetic!" Connor moaned. MB2 was a state-of-the-art, carbon fibre, power-assisted wonder bike – but it was a *little* bit small.

"It's really good in tight places," Connor's mum explained patiently. She was the mechanic at the Pedal-O bike hire shop, where she looked after Connor's amazing top-secret Monster Bikes.

Connor's dog, Trixie, sniffed the wheels. "There's no room for Trixie," Connor grumbled.

Mum pulled open a hatch at the back of the bike. "Yes, there is!"

"There's no room for sandwiches!" Connor was not happy with the new bike.

"I've made you nice, small sandwiches," Mum smiled.

"They're not proper sandwiches!"
Connor complained.

"They fit perfectly under the saddle,"
said Mum. "Anyway, you should be
grateful to have any sandwiches at all.
It's hard enough to get bread since the
baker left town."

Just then, Connor's MiPod beeped.

MiPod XL

MISSION ALERT!

To: Monster Boy,
Number One Agent

From: Mission Control,
Ministry of Monsters

Subject: An Ogre is on the
rampage in the Dark Hills

He's not getting his daily bread and it's
making him grumpy.

Please investigate immediately.
Be careful – he's very irritable.

Good luck!

M.O.M.

**THIS MESSAGE WILL
SELF-ERASE IN
FIFTEEN SECONDS**

"I know how the Ogre feels," Connor muttered, as he climbed into the saddle of MB2.

"Wait a second." Mum pressed a button on MB2. "This is the really good bit."

A small electronic screen popped up on the handlebars.

"Satellite Navigation!" she announced.

That got Connor's attention. "Wow! That's amazing! Come on, Trix, get your helmet on. We can try it out right now!"

The Sat Nav unit plotted a route to the Dark Hills.

Dark Hills

MiPod XL

MISSION UPDATE

The Dark Hills

The Dark Hills were the site of ancient iron mining over one thousand years ago.

Magnetic forces in the iron are powerful enough to slow down watches and affect electronic equipment.

Radios in the area can only pick up Russian pop music stations!

M.O.M.

"It will be a good test," Connor's mum said. "But make sure you stick to the path and follow the route on the Sat Nav."

She looked nervous as she waved goodbye to her son. Not everyone who went into the Dark Hills came out again!

"Don't worry, Mum, I'll be fine!" Connor yelled as he pedalled off.

Connor's mum was a Gargoyle, so Connor was half-monster. His code-name was Monster Boy. If anyone could look after himself, Connor could.

The Dark Hills looked like their name sounded. Hundreds of small, dark-red hills created a tangled web of narrow paths between them.

Trixie leant out of her hatch, took in the view and growled a warning.

"The Sat Nav says go straight ahead. We can't get lost." Connor reassured her. "Hold on tight. Here we go!"

Mum had been right. On the tight, narrow pathways, MB2 steered like a dream.

Soon, they were right in the middle of the maze of hills. *Haven't we passed that tree before?* Connor wondered.

A minute later he skidded to a halt. "That's the third time we've passed this tree." Connor tapped the Sat Nav gently. The map swung round on the screen. It pointed in a different direction.

"Oh, great! We're lost!"

Connor's MiPod beeped. At least that was working.

"It's a message from Dad!" said Connor.

Connor's dad was Gary O'Goyle, the world-famous Mountain Bike Champion. He always sent messages at the most unhelpful times!

Hi son,

Having a great time at the All Ireland Mountain Bike Challenge. Great to be back home, staying with your granny. She sends her love. Here's a picture of us having a picnic!

Lots of love,
Dad

"Oh, great!" said Connor. "No bread shortage there!"

Trixie barked and stared into the distance. She'd heard something.

Soon Connor heard it too. A slow dragging thump of heavy feet on the soft ground. Then a rasping, booming voice filled the air:

"Fee! Fi! Fo! Fum! I smell the blood of an Englishman! Be he alive or be he dead, I'll grind his bones to make my bread!"

"It's the Ogre!" Connor squeaked. "He doesn't sound very happy!"

Connor slammed MB2 into power-assist mode and screeched off down the path, spraying mud and leaves behind him.

Connor felt the thud of heavy footsteps through the ultra-light, carbon fibre bike frame. The Sat Nav map swung round in manic circles. It was useless. Connor had no idea which way to go!

"Raaar!" The Ogre loomed out of nowhere, blocking the path.

He was behind me a second ago! Connor thought as he slammed the bike into a half-brake skid. However scared he was, Connor couldn't help but be impressed with the way the bike handled!

MONSTER BIKE INFO
MB2

The small, carbon fibre body of MB2 works best in narrow and twisty environments.

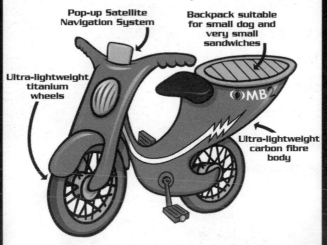

Pop-up Satellite Navigation System

Backpack suitable for small dog and very small sandwiches

Ultra-lightweight titanium wheels

Ultra-lightweight carbon fibre body

The MB2 Sat Nav shows the current location by using up to seven orbiting satellites. It can be confused by strong magnetic forces.

Pop-up Sat Nav

The Ogre waved a large,
knobbly club above his
large, knobbly head. His
teeth were broken and
green with scum. Stiff,
bristly hairs poked out of
his ears. His nostrils flared
in his piggy-like snout.

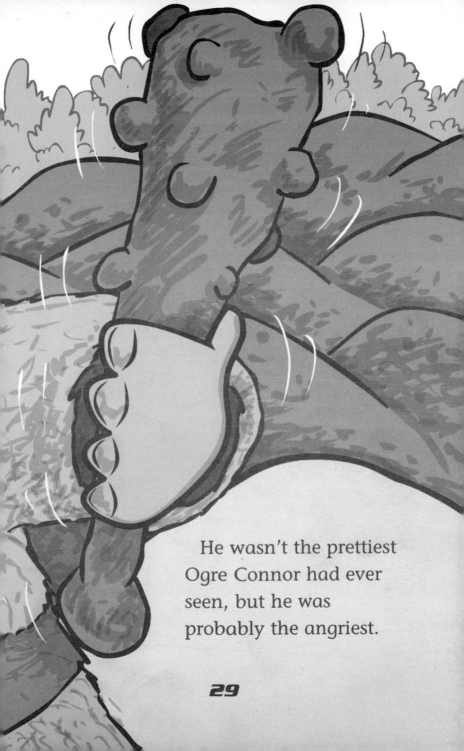

He wasn't the prettiest
Ogre Connor had ever
seen, but he was
probably the angriest.

Trixie barked wildly as the Ogre's huge, lumbering footsteps brought him closer and closer. The air filled with his constant, growling chant.

Connor shifted into fifteenth gear. The pedals stiffened. His calf muscles tensed. He gripped the handlebars tightly, slipping and sliding his amazing new bike through ninety-degree turns. He was accelerating faster than any other bike could have managed on the pathways of the lonely Dark Hills.

But it was no use. He could feel the Ogre's hand almost upon him. He was exhausted. His aching body was powerless. The path was too steep. He was finished!

Trixie barked and snapped at the giant hand that yanked Connor out of the saddle.

The Ogre held Connor up by the back of his trousers. He licked his lips and smiled.

"Fee! Fi! Fo! Fum! I smell the blood of an Englishman!" the Ogre laughed, showering Connor in yellow spit and foul breath.

"Be he alive or be he dead, I'll grind his bones to—"

An idea popped into Connor's head.
"Actually," he said, "I'm half-Irish."
"Huh?" The Ogre looked confused.

"Yeah..." Connor tried playing it cool,
"...and my mum's a Gargoyle!"

"Garrr–goyle!" the Ogre yelped.
"Gargoyles taste disgusting." He let go
of Connor as if he were poison. Then
he looked at Trixie and smiled. "Dog
is good!"

Trixie unfurled her wings and flew to the top of a tree.

"Hmmm!" the Ogre grumbled. "Not proper dog!"

"Would you like to share my sandwiches?" Connor asked casually.

"Mmmm!" the Ogre smiled. "Bread!"

MiPOD MONSTER IDENTIFIER PROGRAM

Monster:	
Ogre	

Distinguishing Features:
Knobbly head, hairy ears, filthy teeth.

Preferred Habitat:
Caves.

Essential Information:
Ogres are all noise and no action. However, they like to keep up their fearsome reputation so they might pretend to eat you. Ogres usually live quietly in their caves, cooking, cleaning and sewing. They do not like to be disturbed.

Danger Rating: 4

"So, which do you prefer?" Connor asked as he handed the Ogre one of his tiny sandwiches. "Grinding bones or eating bread?"

"Mmmm! Bread!" the Ogre growled happily, as he popped the tiny sandwich into his huge, dribbling mouth. "Mmmm – good!"

"If you show me the way out of here," Connor bargained, "I've got an idea that you might just be interested in!"

A few weeks later, Connor and his mum were finishing their shopping in the supermarket.

"I wonder if they've got any bread for your sandwiches?" said Mum.

"Mmmm! Monster bread!" Connor roared in an Ogre-ish sort of way. He pointed to a display of giant-sized loaves of bread.

There was an enormous,
cardboard cut-out of the Ogre,
with a sign that said:

NEW!
MONSTER BREAD
Baked fresh every
day by your local
friendly Ogre.

Mum raised her eyebrows. "You'll need a much bigger bike if you want sandwiches that size," she joked.

Connor smiled sweetly. "It's funny you should say that...I've been meaning to talk to you about a bigger bike!"

SHOO RAYNER

MONSTER BOY

Dino Destroyer	978 1 40830 248 4
Mummy Menace	978 1 40830 249 1
Dragon Danger	978 1 40830 250 7
Werewolf Wail	978 1 40830 251 4
Gorgon Gaze	978 1 40830 252 1
Ogre Outrage	978 1 40830 253 8
Siren Spell	978 1 40830 254 5
Minotaur Maze	978 1 40830 255 2

All priced at £3.99

The Monster Boy stories are available from all good bookshops,
or can be ordered direct from the publisher:
Orchard Books, PO BOX 29, Douglas IM99 1BQ
Credit card orders please telephone 01624 836000
or fax 01624 837033 or visit our website: www.orchardbooks.co.uk
or e-mail: bookshop@enterprise.net for details.

To order please quote title, author and ISBN
and your full name and address.
Cheques and postal orders should be made payable to 'Bookpost plc.'
Postage and packing is FREE within the UK
(overseas customers should add £2.00 per book).

Prices and availability are subject to change.